Congratulations on choosing the best in educational materials for your child. By selecting top-quality McGraw-Hill products, you can be assured that the concepts used in our books will reinforce and enhance the skills that are being taught in classrooms nationwide.

And what better way to get young readers excited than with Mercer Mayer's Little Critter, a character loved by children everywhere? Our First Readers offer simple and engaging stories about Little Critter that children can read on their own. Each level incorporates reading skills, colorful illustrations, and challenging activities.

Level 1 – The stories are simple and use repetitive language. Illustrations are highly supportive.
Level 2 - The stories begin to grow in complexity. Language is still repetitive, but it is mixed with more challenging vocabulary.
Level 3 - The stories are more complex. Sentences are longer and more varied.

To help your child make the most of this book, look at the first few pictures in the story and discuss what is happening. Ask your child to predict where the story is going. Then, once your child has read the story, have him or her review the word list and do the activities. This will reinforce vocabulary words from the story and build reading comprehension.

You are your child's first and most influential teacher. No one knows your child the way you do. Tailor your time together to reinforce a newly acquired skill or to overcome a temporary stumbling block. Praise your child's progress and ideas, take delight in his or her imagination, and most of all, enjoy your time together!

McGraw-Hill
Children's Publishing

Send all inquiries to:
McGraw-Hill Children's Publishing
8787 Orion Place
Columbus, OH 43240-4027

Printed in the United States of America.

1-57768-846-5

 A Big Tuna Trading Company, LLC/J. R. Sansevere Book

Library of Congress Cataloging-in-Publication Data is on file with the publisher.

1 2 3 4 5 6 7 8 9 10 PHXBK 07 06 05 04 03 02

EAS

FIRST READERS

Level **2**   Grades **K–1**

GRANDMA'S GARDEN

by Mercer Mayer

McGraw-Hill
Children's Publishing

Columbus, Ohio

Today, we are going to help
Grandma plant a garden.
I picked out a bunch of seeds.
Little Sister did too.

SHOVE

STICKS

GOOD
DIRT

4

First, we dug rows in the ground.
I used a hoe.
Little Sister used a shovel.

Next, we planted our seeds.
I planted peas and carrots.

Little Sister planted beans.

10

Every day, we worked on the garden.
I watered the plants.
Little Sister pulled weeds.

We watched the plants . . .

. . . grow bigger and bigger.

13

By the end of the summer,
it was time to pick our vegetables.

15

Grandma said this was
her best garden ever.
I said I never knew
vegetables could be so yummy!

17

Word List

Read each word in the lists below. Then, find each word in the story. Now, make up a new sentence using the word. Say your sentence out loud.

Words I Know	Challenge Words
plant	shovel
seeds	watched
peas	vegetables
carrots	knew
beans	
garden	
weeds	

Describing Words

Little Critter has made a list of words to describe himself.

young   smart

nice   happy

Here are some more describing words. Point to the words that best describe the vegetables in the basket.

orange   furry   green

happy   crunchy   purple

smart   brown

friendly

yummy

Words Ending with -ed

To make most action words tell about something that happened in the past, add ed to the end of the word.

Example: plant   planted

If the action word ends in e, then just add a d.

Examples:

like   liked

use   used

rake   raked

raise   raised

Read the sentences and decide if the action is happening now or in the past. Point to the correct answer.

I rake leaves.   Now or In the Past

Grandpa mowed   Now or In the Past
the grass.

We worked hard.   Now or In the Past

We pull weeds.   Now or In the Past

I pick beans.   Now or In the Past

Little Sister sprayed   Now or In the Past
the hose.

The Word I

When you write about yourself, use the word I. Always write I with a capital letter.

Example: I planted seeds.

When you write about yourself and someone else, always put the other person first.

Example: Little Sister and I took care of the garden.

Read the pairs of sentences below and the ones on the next page. Point to the sentence in each pair that uses I correctly.

Grandma and I picked berries.

I and Grandma picked berries.

I and Grandma baked pies.

Grandma and I baked pies.

Grandpa and I milked the cow.

I and Grandpa milked the cow.

I and Little Sister watched the sheep.

Little Sister and I watched the sheep.

Answer Key

page 19
Describing Words

(orange)   furry   (green)

happy   (crunchy) (purple)

smart   (brown)

friendly

(yummy)

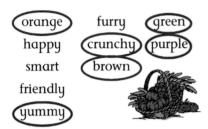

page 21
Words Ending with -ed

I rake leaves.	(Now) or In the Past
Grandpa mowed the grass.	Now or (In the Past)
We worked hard.	Now or (In the Past)
We pull weeds.	(Now) or In the Past
I pick beans.	(Now) or In the Past
Little Sister sprayed the hose.	Now or (In the Past)

page 22
The Word I

(Grandma and I picked berries.)

I and Grandma picked berries.

page 23
The Word I

I and Grandma baked pies.

(Grandma and I baked pies.)

(Grandpa and I milked the cow.)

I and Grandpa milked the cow.

I and Little Sister watched the sheep.

(Little Sister and I watched the sheep.)